CLASSICS ✦ RETOLD

D0176865

20,000 Leagues Under The Sea

TULLAMORE MAY 2023 WITHDRAWN

RETOLD BY
LYNNE BENTON

ILLUSTRATED BY
ALEK SOTIROVSKI

LONDON • SYDNEY

Leabharlann
Chontae Uíbh Fhailí

Class:

Acc:

Inv:

First published in 2011 by
Franklin Watts
338 Euston Road
London NW1 3BH

Franklin Watts Australia
Level 17/207 Kent Street
Sydney NSW 2000

Text © Franklin Watts 2011
Illustrations by Alex Sotirovski © Franklin Watts 2011
Cover design by Peter Scoulding

The author and illustrator have asserted their rights in accordance
with the Copyright, Designs and Patents Act, 1988.

All rights reserved. No part of this publication may be
reproduced, stored in a retrieval system, or transmitted
in any form or by any means, electronic, mechanical,
photocopy, recording or otherwise, without the prior
written permission of the copyright owner.

A CIP catalogue record for this book
is available from the British Library.

ISBN: 978 1 4451 0461 4

Dewey Classification: 823.9'2

3 5 7 9 10 8 6 4 2

Printed in Great Britain

Franklin Watts is a division of Hachette Children's Books,
an Hachette UK company.
www.hachette.co.uk

For Tobias

Contents

Chapter One
The sea monster

My adventure began in New York in the summer of 1886. There had been several shipwrecks over the last few months. Some people were beginning to think that a mysterious sea monster had caused them. They said it was a huge black creature with glowing eyes, but others laughed at the idea.

"What do you think, Professor Aronnax?" people asked me. "You're the expert. Do you think there's a monster down there?"

"I don't know what to think," I said. Although I'd studied underwater life for many years, I'd never heard of such a thing.

Then I was asked to join an expedition to catch the monster before it did any more damage. Of course I accepted, and my faithful assistant, Conseil, came too. And soon we were sailing away on what was to be the most memorable journey of my life.

The ship's captain had promised a reward to the person who spotted the monster, so all the sailors were desperate to win. All except Ned Land, the only Canadian on board. He was an expert harpooner, and didn't believe in mysterious monsters.

We sailed for weeks with no sign of it, until even the captain was ready to give up.

Suddenly Ned shouted, "Monster ahead!"

Everyone rushed to the side of the ship in time to see a long black shape just under the water, rushing towards us. It looked like a great black fish with no fins or tail, and its eyes glowed. I was leaning over to see better when the ship gave a great lurch and I fell overboard.

The shock of the cold water stopped my brain from working. I couldn't swim. I couldn't breathe. As I plunged down into the inky darkness I thought my last moment had come.

Then someone grabbed me and I felt myself being pulled up until my head broke the surface of the water.

As I gasped for air I saw that my rescuer was my assistant, Conseil.

"Conseil!" I spluttered. "Did you fall too?"

"No, I jumped in to save you," panted Conseil. "But the ship has gone!"

He was right. I saw to my despair that the ship was heading back the way we had come. It had a large hole in its side. We were alone in an unfriendly sea, miles from any shore, and somewhere nearby was an angry sea monster, waiting for its next meal...

"I am grateful to you, Conseil," I said. "But now we shall both drown."

Just then we heard a shout.

"Over here!" called a voice. We turned our heads and saw Ned Land. He seemed to be standing on the surface of the sea. He was holding his harpoon and grinning at us.

We swam towards him. Then we saw to our amazement that he was standing on the back of the monster. As its long black shape rose slowly out of the water, we gasped in horror.

But Ned said, "This is no monster! Its scales are made of cast iron!"

Chapter Two
The Nautilus

Ned reached out and pulled us both up beside him onto the iron back of the 'monster'.

"You see?" he said. "It's a submarine!"

"A submarine?" I echoed. "You mean a ship that can travel underwater? But I thought they only existed in stories!"

Suddenly a hatch beside us slid open, and several men climbed out. Without a word they grabbed us and dragged us down inside the submarine. We were too shocked to resist.

They bundled us into a small cabin. It was clean and well-lit, but as they closed the door behind us we heard the key turn in the lock.

"We're trapped!" said Ned.

But as we wondered what would happen to us now, the door opened again and another man walked in. He had black hair and a great black beard, and his eyes were dark and piercing.

"Good morning," he said. "Welcome aboard the *Nautilus*. My name is Captain Nemo."

"Good morning," I said. "I am..," but I got no further.

"I know who you are, Professor Aronnax," said Captain Nemo. "You have quite a reputation. I have all of your books in my library."

The other two introduced themselves, and Ned said, "This is a great submarine, Captain. We are truly impressed. But we want to know how soon we can leave."

Captain Nemo looked at him steadily.

Then he said, "I'm afraid that won't be possible, Mr Land. You are my guests, but you are also my prisoners." Captain Nemo went on, "I don't intend you to starve. We live well down here. My men will call you when your meal is ready."

With that he went out of the cabin, closing the door behind him. Ned rushed to the door and tried it, but it was locked again.

Suddenly all the lights in the cabin went off, and we were plunged into darkness.

"Now what?" growled Ned.

Then we heard a grinding sound, and one wall began to slide open to reveal a window. In the lights from the *Nautilus* we saw a fantastic underwater world.

There were strange, exotic sea creatures I'd only seen in pictures. There were seahorses and starfish, and beautiful pink sea plants waving their fronds. And so many different species of fish! I could hardly speak for excitement.

"Fish!" snorted Ned. "Nothing but fish!"

I stared at him. "But they're amazing!" I said. "Those blue ones, for instance —"

"Professor, I like my fish on a plate, with chips," said Ned. "What really matters is how we're going to get out of here!"

Chapter Three
Captain Nemo

Soon the light in the cabin went back on and the wall slid shut again. Then the door opened and one of the silent crew took us into a large cabin, where a table was set for four people. As we sat down, Captain Nemo joined us.

The meal was the most delicious I had ever eaten. There was fish, of course, but also some exotic foods I had never tasted before. I could only guess what they were.

"This is amazing, Captain," I said, after a few mouthfuls. "Where does it all come from?"

"From the sea," said Captain Nemo. "Everything on board comes from under the sea. It is a wonderful place. You will soon get to love it, too."

Ned was about to argue, but I thought it would be wise to keep on the right side of the mysterious Captain.

"May we see round your ship?" I asked.

Captain Nemo smiled. "Of course."

So we all followed him on a tour of the
Nautilus.

It was surprisingly comfortable. As well as
the kitchens and the engine rooms, there
were a big sitting room, a music room and a
well-stocked library.

"You are welcome to read my books,
Professor," said the Captain.

"Thank you," I said. "May I ask how you keep enough fresh air on board?"

"Every twenty-four hours we go to the surface to take in a day's supply," he said. "Now let me show you to your cabins."

We had separate cabins, which again were comfortable. But nothing changed the fact that we were prisoners.

For the next few days we didn't see Captain Nemo at all. Ned grumbled, but I was fascinated by the views of the undersea world, and welcomed the chance to read so many books on the subject. Conseil helped me list all the fish we saw, and I began to write a journal. When we got home I wanted to have a record of our voyage.

I still didn't quite believe that we were prisoners. Surely Captain Nemo would let us go soon? I couldn't make up my mind about him. In some ways I admired him and wanted to trust him, and yet...

One day he came to my cabin and said, "Professor, would you care to come for a walk with me?"

I thought he was joking. I laughed. "A walk? Where? On the sea bed?"

"Yes," said Captain Nemo, quite seriously.

"Oh!" I said. "Yes, please."

The Captain asked me to follow him, and

he led me into a chamber we hadn't seen before. There he handed me a suit of some leathery fabric and told me to put it on, while he put on an identical one. He gave me a round glass helmet, like a goldfish bowl, for my head, and a large pack for my back. He said the pack contained oxygen so that I would be able to breathe underwater. Then he led me into a sealed chamber containing a small raised pool filled with seawater, and when Captain Nemo jumped into it, I followed him.

Chapter Four
The underwater world

It was an incredible experience, walking along the sea bed, and the oxygen tank allowed me to breathe normally.

I wanted to stop and look at everything. It was hard to believe I could actually walk among the fish, over rocks encrusted with strange sea creatures, and through waving fronds of sea plants.

Ahead of us I could see something that looked like trees, but whoever heard of trees growing underwater? I wished I could ask Captain Nemo about them, but with our helmets on he couldn't hear me, nor I him.

At last Captain Nemo indicated that we should get back to the *Nautilus*. Reluctantly, I followed him, but I will never forget the thrill of my first under-water walk.

After that there were other underwater expeditions, which I very much enjoyed.

Sometimes we came across wrecked ships. I couldn't help wondering with a shiver if, like our ship, they had been attacked by the *Nautilus*, on Captain Nemo's orders.

But most of the time we spent on board, wondering when we would be allowed to leave.

Then one day, as we travelled underwater, we heard a strange juddering sound, and the *Nautilus* stopped moving.

"What's happened?" Ned asked.

A moment later Captain Nemo strode into the sitting room. "I apologise for the interruption to our journey," he said. "We have run aground on a coral reef. I'm afraid we will have to stay here until the tide floats us off again."

"You mean there's land here?" asked Ned in excitement.

Captain Nemo nodded. "There is a small island," he said. "You may, if you wish, go ashore and see it for yourselves. But I warn you, it may not be as welcoming as you hope."

"I don't care," said Ned. "I just want to go ashore!"

As we reached the hatch, for the first time I noticed that something was fastened to the underside. It was a small dinghy. I pointed it out to Ned, but at that moment he was more interested in getting out.

We scrambled up through the hatch and stood again on the iron back of the *Nautilus*, breathing in the wonderful fresh air. A little way off stood an island, with sand and palm trees and rocks and grass.

"Look at that!" breathed Ned. "Land! Freedom!"

We all dived into the sea and swam the short distance to the shore. There Conseil and I picked coconuts and fruits from the trees, while Ned went hunting for anything he could find for our supper.

Soon he came back with his kill, so we built a fire and started cooking.

"Meat at last!" said Ned, with a grin.

We stretched out, full of our lunch and happy to be outside.

The next moment, a big stone landed at my feet. It was closely followed by another, and then another.

Chapter Five
Attack!

We looked up, alarmed, and saw that we were surrounded by glaring natives with more stones in their hands.

We left our picnic and raced down to the water's edge. Then we swam as fast as we could back to the *Nautilus*!

Just as we reached the submarine, however, Ned looked over his shoulder, and shouted, "They're coming after us!"

We yanked the hatch open and almost slid down the steps in our haste to escape the angry natives. "Quick!" I cried. "Shut the hatch! They mustn't get in!"

Conseil shut the hatch, but our pursuers were already nearly upon us.

"We must tell Captain Nemo," I said. "He'll know what to do."

But to our surprise, Captain Nemo was quite calm. "Don't worry," he said. "They won't trouble us."

At that moment we heard footsteps overhead, as the natives climbed all over the *Nautilus*. Then we heard one trying the hatch. To our horror he wrenched it open.

"Captain Nemo!" I cried. "They're coming into the sub!"

Captain Nemo shook his head. "I told you not to worry," he said, and he flicked a switch I had never noticed before. Instantly there was a yell from the man at the top of the steps. Then another yelled, and another, and then before we knew it all the men had leapt into the sea and started swimming back to shore.

I frowned. "What did you do?" I asked.

Captain Nemo smiled. "I just turned on the electricity supply," he said. "All the rails around the hatch are electrified to deter trespassers. It won't kill them – after all, you invaded their island – but it will stop them trying to board us again."

We were still shaking at our narrow escape when we felt the *Nautilus* lurch, and once again we were floating.

"You see," said Captain Nemo. "The tide has floated us off the reef, just as I said."

After that we didn't mention escaping for a while. Even Ned seemed to have given up on the idea for now as the *Nautilus* journeyed on.

One night I was about to get ready for bed when Captain Nemo knocked on my cabin door.

"You might like to see this, Professor," he said. "Come with me."

I did as he asked, and once again we put on our diving suits. Then he said, "This is a long trip, and we shall be going far from the lights of the *Nautilus*. But it's worth it, as you will find out."

I was puzzled, but followed him along the sea bed until we were well beyond the *Nautilus*. But way ahead of us was a red glow that lit up the sea for miles around. I became even more curious.

The ground was rocky and sloped steeply upwards, so the journey was hard going. But as we reached the top of the slope I looked down and saw at last where the glow was coming from.

Chapter Six
The lost city

I was looking into the heart of an underwater volcano.

I had never imagined that such a thing existed. The brilliant light came from the red-hot lava pouring from its mouth.

And at its foot was something even more amazing. A whole city lay spread out before us with towers, gold temples, bridges, streets and houses, but every bit of it underwater. I stood and stared, but the Captain was already leading the way down into its streets.

He stopped and picked up a piece of slate from the sea bed. He scratched one word on it with a stone, and showed it to me.

The word was ATLANTIS.

I gasped. Everyone had heard of the lost city of Atlantis, which was said to have been drowned in a flood thousands of years ago. But nobody believed it really existed.

I couldn't believe I was actually walking along Atlantis's long-lost streets. It was well worth the long journey to see it.

When we got back to the *Nautilus* I thanked Captain Nemo, but he just smiled and said goodnight. By then I was so tired that I slept for most of the next morning.

When I awoke I told my friends about the lost city, but they didn't seem interested.

"Do you know where we're heading next?" growled Ned. "The South Pole!"

"The South Pole?" I echoed in disbelief. "But there's only ice there!"

"Captain Nemo says we'll be travelling under the ice," said Ned gloomily. "So there'll be no chance to escape."

By the time we reached the South Pole even the air inside the *Nautilus* felt a lot colder. When we saw the vast expanse of ice all

around us I was amazed that Captain Nemo
had managed to steer a course through all
the icebergs. When the Sun shone they were
beautiful, but I realised that we were in a
dangerous position. What would happen if
the icebergs moved?

And that was exactly what happened, two days later. The iceberg in front of us shifted and blocked our passage forward, and as we prepared to turn and go back, the iceberg behind us moved into the gap. We were trapped!

"Now what are we going to do?" Ned demanded.

"It's perfectly simple," Captain Nemo said. "We shall go under the ice."

"But they say that seven-eighths of an iceberg is below the waterline," I said. "Suppose it's blocking our way down as well?"

"Then we shall just have to chip our way through it," said Captain Nemo calmly.

I hoped for all our sakes that this wouldn't be necessary.

Chapter Seven
Under the ice

At first all was well. We sank down and down until we were well below the surface of the water, and I began to think we really could go underneath the iceberg.

Then disaster struck. With a great jolt, the *Nautilus* suddenly stopped moving. The Captain hurried forward to the engine room, and returned a few minutes later, looking worried.

"We've run aground on the base of the iceberg," he said. "But another ice shelf has shifted and now lies above us. So we can't move up or down."

"So we'll have to chip our way through the ice?" I asked.

Captain Nemo nodded. "But there's a problem," he said. "We can't get to the surface for fresh air, and what we've got on board will only last a day or two at the most.

After that..." He shook his head.

"Then we'll have to work quickly," I said.
"We'll all help. Ned is strong. He'll get us
through the ice in no time."

Captain Nemo gave a grim smile. "Let's
hope so," he said.

By now the crew were in their diving suits,
with oxygen packs on their backs. They took
the first shift, and hacked at the ice with
pickaxes until Captain Nemo ordered them
back on board. Then he and the three of us
took over.

Between us we worked all day and all night, and our supply of fresh air grew less and less. By the following day the remaining air on board was so thin and bad that we could hardly breathe. But we knew we mustn't stop, so we worked even faster.

Finally, just as our lungs were about to burst, we broke through the last piece of ice. To our huge relief the *Nautilus* dived down under the iceberg and rose swiftly to the surface on the other side.

Then we all went up through the hatch to take deep breaths of cold, fresh air. We were safe.

But Ned was angry.

"He risked all our lives by his stupid idea of coming to the South Pole!" he said. "We've got to escape!"

After what we'd just been through, even I agreed with him.

"But not here," I said. "It's far too cold. We must wait till we get into warmer seas."

Chapter Eight
The giant squid

It took us a while to travel back towards the Equator, but there it was too hot to escape. And we couldn't help noticing that every time Captain Nemo surfaced for air, we were a long way from land.

"Wait till we get nearer home," I said. "Then if necessary we'll swim for it!"

Ned grinned. "There's always the dinghy."

But before we reached anywhere near home, another disaster struck. This time it came from under the sea itself.

We suddenly realised that although the engines were running, we weren't moving. Then the wall of the cabin slid back to reveal a huge eye staring in through the window.

We all drew back in horror. "What is it?" asked Conseil shakily.

At that moment Captain Nemo came in.

"We've been attacked," he said. "A giant squid has wrapped its tentacles around our rudder, so we can't move. And now it's dragging us up to the surface."

Ned brightened. "No problem," he said. "I've still got my harpoon, and I'm good at killing things like this."

Captain Nemo frowned. "It may not be that easy," he said. "This squid is huge – far bigger than any you may have met before."

"I said I'll deal with it," said Ned, and before anyone could stop him he was up the steps and pushing open the hatch.

A terrifying sight met our eyes. A great pink squid, ten times bigger than anything I'd ever seen, was squatting on the *Nautilus*, its tentacles wrapped around it. The moment the hatch opened, one of its tentacles slapped down the steps.

But Ned dodged it, and in no time he was charging at the creature with his harpoon, trying to stab it between its huge, staring

eyes. The squid grew angrier and angrier,
and when it wrapped its tentacles around
him I was afraid it would squeeze him to
death. But at that moment Ned yanked
himself free. Then, with all his strength,
he stabbed the creature between the eyes.
A spurt of some dark liquid – the creature's
blood, I supposed – shot into the air, but for

a moment nothing else happened. Then the squid slid slowly off the *Nautilus* and sank down into the depths of the sea.

"You are a hero, Ned," said the Captain.

Ned liked that, and for the next day or so he said nothing about leaving. But then we saw something else that made us more determined than ever to escape.

Chapter 9
Whirlpool!

One morning we saw a huge warship
bearing down on us. I thought we would just
dive down and let it go on, but Captain
Nemo had other ideas.

"Sink it!" he barked.

I couldn't believe my ears. Surely he didn't
mean it? But as we watched in horror, the
Nautilus rammed the warship again and
again, leaving a huge hole in its side. The
ship tipped over and then slowly sank to the
bottom of the sea, with all its men on board.

I turned to him, trembling with shock. "Why did you do that?" I demanded. "What had they done to you?"

"Warships killed my wife and my family, and destroyed my country," snarled Captain Nemo. "I will never rest until I have destroyed them too."

And with that he strode out of the room.

"He's crazy!" said Ned. "We've got to leave now, before he decides to destroy us as well!"

I nodded. "I agree," I said. "As soon as we see land, we'll go."

But then the *Nautilus* seemed to put on extra speed, and before we knew it we were rushing towards the North Pole.

"If we don't leave soon we'll be caught in icebergs again!" said Ned.

"Tonight," I promised. "Whatever happens, we'll go tonight!"

"We'll take the dinghy," said Ned.

So that night we all put on our warmest clothes, and I put my journal in my pocket.

Then, trying not to wake up Captain Nemo or the crew, we crept up towards the hatch.

Conseil began to unscrew the dinghy. When there was only one bolt left to go, we all climbed in and I opened the hatch above us. But as I did so a ferocious wind whipped at our clothes and almost swept us overboard. We clung on tightly, hoping Conseil would manage to free the dinghy quickly.

But as he struggled with the final bolt, I turned and saw a terrifying sight. The wind had whipped up the sea into a giant whirlpool, huge, fast-moving and deadly. Already the *Nautilus* was caught up in its outer ring, and we were all being sucked down into the centre.

At that moment, with a great snap the remaining bolt sheared off, and the dinghy shot into the edge of the whirlpool.

Then everything went black.

When I came to, I was lying on the floor
of a fisherman's hut with my two friends
beside me. The fisherman said he'd found
us washed up on the shore, but with no sign
of the dinghy, or any other vessel. Although
we were amazed that we'd survived the
dreadful whirlpool, we wondered about the
Nautilus. What had happened to it, and to
Captain Nemo?

Even all these years later, I have no idea.

Jules Verne (1828–1905)

Jules Verne was born in Brittany in France on 8 February 1828. He was fascinated by exploration from an early age, and once tried to stow away on a boat to the Caribbean!

Verne's other lifelong passions were science and writing. At school, he started writing short stories that explored all of his great loves – quirky tales of adventurous journeys, that were rich in geographic and scientific detail. On leaving school however, his family encouraged him to follow a more

Jules Verne in 1870

stable career, and Verne trained as a lawyer.

Verne combined writing with the law for a while, but soon tired of it and decided to devote himself to his writing. In 1863, he finally published his first novel – a story about balloon exploration in Africa. Many other celebrated works, including *20,000 Leagues Under the Sea*, soon followed.

Over a hundred years after his death, Verne is still one of the most popular and most translated authors in the world. He is often hailed as the father of science fiction, for he had the gift of making science accessible to all in his writing.

20,000 Leagues Under the Sea (1869)

20,000 Leagues Under the Sea is one of Verne's best-known and best-loved stories. It shows Verne's dazzling scientific imagination, for submarines had not been invented when he wrote the book, while scuba equipment was not widely used until the 1930s. Verne didn't get everything right, however. At the depths to which the *Nautilus* dived, water pressure would have crushed both the sub and the crew instantly!

Titles in the CLASSICS RETOLD series:

978 1 4451 0461 4 PB
978 1 4451 0818 6 eBook

978 1 4451 0460 7 PB
978 1 4451 0815 5 eBook

978 1 4451 0458 4 PB
978 1 4451 0819 3 eBook

978 1 4451 0462 1 PB
978 1 4451 0817 9 eBook

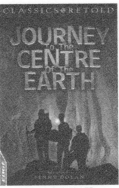

978 1 4451 0459 1 PB
978 1 4451 0816 2 eBook

978 1 4451 0457 7 PB
978 1 4451 0820 9 eBook